ROCKET POWER

AVALANCHE TRAIL

by **Terry Collins**

illustrated by
Paul Windle Design Ltd.

Simon Spotlight/Nickelodeon

New York   London   Toronto   Sydney   Singapore

Based on the TV series *Nickelodeon Rocket Power*™ created by Klasky Csupo, Inc. as seen on Nickelodeon®

SIMON SPOTLIGHT
An imprint of Simon & Schuster Children's Publishing Division
1230 Avenue of the Americas, New York, New York 10020

Manufactured in the United States of America
First Edition   10 9 8 7 6 5 4 3 2 1
ISBN 0-689-84987-7

"Mountainboarding rocks, Dad! Wait until you see me busting a frontside 180," Otto said as they headed to Mt. Baldy.

"Uh, a frontside what?" asked Ray.

"It's when you turn the tail of your board into a nose roll," Otto said.

"It's totally cool," said Twister, high-fiving Otto.

Ray laughed. "Give me the salty spray of the ocean," he said. "Hanging ten off the nose of a surfboard . . . now that's *my* idea of a thrill."

"A surfer supreme like you would make a wicked mountainboarder, Dad,"
Reggie said. "You should hit the trails with us."
"Please, Mr. Rocket? It would be fun!" Sam agreed.
"Okay, why not?" Ray said with a grin.

Otto rushed ahead of everyone. "You need to chill and wait for Dad," Reggie called.

"I'll see him at the bottom," Otto replied. "I want to check out the new trail that shakes out the wanna-bes from the board kings!"

"You mean A-a-avalanche Trail?" Sam asked.

"Yeah, dude," Otto said. "Twist, you got the camera ready?"

"Hold off on that close-up, Twist," Reggie said. "Avalanche Trail's an advanced ride, bro. Adults only."

Otto flipped his board under one arm and shrugged. "Come on, Rocket girl, I'm a better mountainboarder than any old adult and you know it."

Reggie didn't budge. "Maybe so, but I don't make the rules."

Otto pushed past his sister. "Time to let the panic commence!" he said. "Come on, Twist!"

"You should at least warm up on the shorter routes," Sam cautioned, peeking down the steep trail.

"Don't be lame, Sam," Otto said, hopping back on his board. "Rules were made to be broken!"

Reggie shrugged. "Your choice, dude. Ride on Avalanche Trail and the only thing broken will be your board . . . or your neck."

Sam tapped Reggie on the shoulder. "Come on, let's go find Ray."

"How's the search for the perfect board, Mr. Rocket?" Sam asked when they found him.

"This green beauty will be just the ticket," Ray replied, holding up his newly rented mountainboard.

"Awesome, Dad!" Reggie said. "It looks good on you!"

"Hey, where's Otto and Twister?" Ray asked.

"Umm," Reggie stammered, "they're doing their thing and uh, we're doing ours."

"Well, if you don't mind the old man tagging along, I could use a few pointers," Ray said, balancing on his board.

"You go, Dad!" Reggie yelled as Ray took the lead down a beginner's trail.

"This is a stylie grab, right?" Ray asked, reaching down for the tip of his board.
"Dad, keep the wheels balanced!" Reggie warned.

Ray's board shot up off the ground and Ray went down—hard!

"Guess I'm not a natural, huh?" Ray said. "Maybe I'll stick to surfing . . . makes for softer landings."

On the other side of the mountain Twister and Otto stood at the top of Avalanche Trail.

"Let's hit it, Twist!" Otto said.

Twister focused the video camera. "Looking good, dude. Ready, willing, and able to catch your descent!"

Otto took a deep breath and glided down the path. "Ride the earth, ride the earth," he muttered as the board picked up speed.

Avalanche Trail was no sweat!
"I'm dropping for the bottom!" Otto called out.
"Awesome!" Twister yelled. "I'm getting some great footage!"

"Twist, do a close-up—," Otto began, just as a loose stone caught under his back wheel sending his ride into orbit!

"Stop the tape! Stop the tape!" an embarrassed Otto cried, hitting the ground and rolling into a ditch.

Twister dropped his camera and raced toward Otto not watching where he was going.

"Ow!" he muttered as his elbow banged into a wall.

There was the clacking sound of two rocks hitting together, then stones and dirt began to fall.

"Ugh!" Twister gasped as he was swept away by the newly created landslide. "Help!"

"Uhhh, that was a wicked wipeout," Otto moaned as he got to his feet. "Thanks for the assist, Twist."

Otto paused. "Twist?" He turned as a roaring sound echoed down the trail.

The air became so cloudy with dust that he couldn't see anything!

"Twister? Where are you, man?" Otto shouted, searching frantically.

There was only one thing he could do. "Daaaaad!" he screamed.

Otto sprinted back to the top of the trail where Ray, Reggie, and Sam were waiting. "He's down there somewhere," Otto said trying to fight back tears.

Ray craned his neck down the trail. "We have to tell the safety patrol. I just hope he isn't too hurt!"

"I'll organize a search party," Reggie jumped in.

"Hold up," Sam said, picking up Twister's discarded video camera. "Twister might have left us his location without even knowing it!"

"Twist couldn't have gone far," Sam replied, looking into the viewfinder of the camera. "Good thing he left the camera running!"

"Are you sure this is the spot, Sam?" Otto asked, digging for his lost friend.

"Wait—I think I hear something!" Reggie said. "Move that pile, Dad."

A faint "Aaarrrggh" could be heard from underneath the rubble.

"Jackpot!" Otto said.

Ray leaned down and called to Twister. "Anything broken Twist?"

"No, but I could use a hand outta here," Twister replied.

Ray lifted a bruised and battered Twister to his feet. Twister looked around at the rock slide in disbelief.

"Whoa! Someone dropped the driveway on my head," he said.

"Oh, no, did the landslide bust my cam?" Twister asked.

"No, it's safe," Otto replied, handing the camera over. "Good thing you left it running. It showed us exactly where to search for you. Twistman, I'm so sorry."

"Aw, it was just an accident," Twister replied.

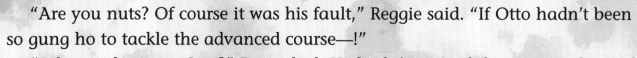

"Are you nuts? Of course it was his fault," Reggie said. "If Otto hadn't been so gung ho to tackle the advanced course—!"

"Advanced course, Otto?" Ray asked. He hadn't noticed the sign on the trail.

"I promise I'll never do anything so dumb again!" said Otto.

"Don't make promises you can't keep, Otto," Ray said.

"No prob, Mr. Rocket," Twister said, holding his camera high. "I'll help him keep this one! I've got it on video!"